Oliver Wendell Holme

Dorothy Q

together with, A ballad of the Boston tea party ; & Grandmother's story ...

Oliver Wendell Holme

Dorothy Q
together with, A ballad of the Boston tea party ; & Grandmother's story ...

ISBN/EAN: 9783744769358

Printed in Europe, USA, Canada, Australia, Japan

Cover: Foto ©Andreas Hilbeck / pixelio.de

More available books at **www.hansebooks.com**

Dorothy Q.

Dorothy Q

Together with

A Ballad of the Boston Tea Party
&
Grandmother's Story of Bunker Hill Battle

By Oliver Wendell Holmes

With Illustrations by

Howard Pyle

Boston and New York
Houghton, Mifflin and Company
The Riverside Press, Cambridge
M DCCC XCIII

1874 and 1875,
By OLIVER WENDELL HOLMES.

1892,
By HOUGHTON, MIFFLIN & CO.

The Riverside Press, Cambridge, Mass., U. S. A.
Electrotyped and Printed by H. O. Houghton & Co.

PREFACE

DOROTHY QUINCY, *the subject of the first poem in this volume, was aunt of the first Josiah Quincy, Junior, " that fervid orator who expended his life for the cause of his country, dying on ship-board in sight of home, as he returned from England after hostilities had begun only seven days." She was also the aunt of a second Dorothy Quincy, who became the wife of John Hancock, President of the first Continental Congress.*

The painting hung in the house of my grand-father, Oliver Wendell, which was occupied by British officers before the evacuation of Boston. One of these gentlemen amused himself by stabbing poor Dorothy (the pictured one) as near the right eye as his swordsmanship would serve him to do it. The canvas was so decayed that it became neces-sary to remount the painting, in the process of doing which the hole made by the rapier was lost sight of. I took some photographs of the picture before it was transferred to the new canvas.

The tax on tea, which was considered so odious and led to the act on which A Ballad of the Boston Tea Party is founded, was but a small matter, only two pence in the pound. But it involved a principle of taxation, to which the Colonies would not submit. Their objection was not to the amount, but the claim. The East India Company, however, sent out a number of tea-ships to different American ports, three of them to Boston.

The inhabitants tried to send them back, but in vain. The captains of the ships had consented, if permitted, to return with their cargoes to England, but the consignees refused to discharge them from their obligations, the custom house to give them a clearance for their return, and the governor to grant them a passport for going by the fort. It was easily seen that the tea would be gradually landed from the ships lying so near the town, and that if landed it would be disposed of, and the purpose of establishing the monopoly and raising a revenue effected. To prevent the dreaded consequence, a number of armed men, disguised like Indians, boarded the ships and threw their whole cargoes of tea into the dock. About seventeen persons boarded the ships in Boston harbor, and emptied three hundred and forty-two chests of tea.[1] Among these " Indians" was Major Thomas Mel-

---

[1] Holmes's *Annals of America*, vol. ii. pp. 181-2.

ville, the same who suggested to me the poem, "The Last Leaf."

The story of Bunker Hill battle is told as literally in accordance with the best authorities as it would have been if it had been written in prose instead of in verse. I have often been asked what steeple it was from which the little group I speak of looked upon the conflict. To this I answer that I am not prepared to speak authoritatively, but that the reader may take his choice among all the steeples standing at that time in the northern part of the city. Christ Church in Salem Street is the one I always think of, but I do not insist upon its claim. As to the personages who made up the small company that followed the old corporal, it would be hard to identify them, but by ascertaining where the portrait by Copley is now to be found, some light may be thrown on their personality.

Daniel Malcolm's gravestone, splintered by British bullets, may be seen in the Copp's Hill burial-ground.

O. W. H.

LIST OF ILLVSTRATIONS

9

GRANDMOTHER'S STORY OF BUNKER-HILL
BATTLE

Dorothy Q.

^

Family Portrait

Dorothy Q.

GRANDMOTHER'S mother : her age, I
    guess,
Thirteen summers, or something less ;
Girlish bust, but womanly air ;
Smooth, square forehead, with up-
    rolled hair,
Lips that lover has never kissed ;
Taper fingers and slender wrist ;
Hanging sleeves of stiff brocade ;
So they painted the little maid.

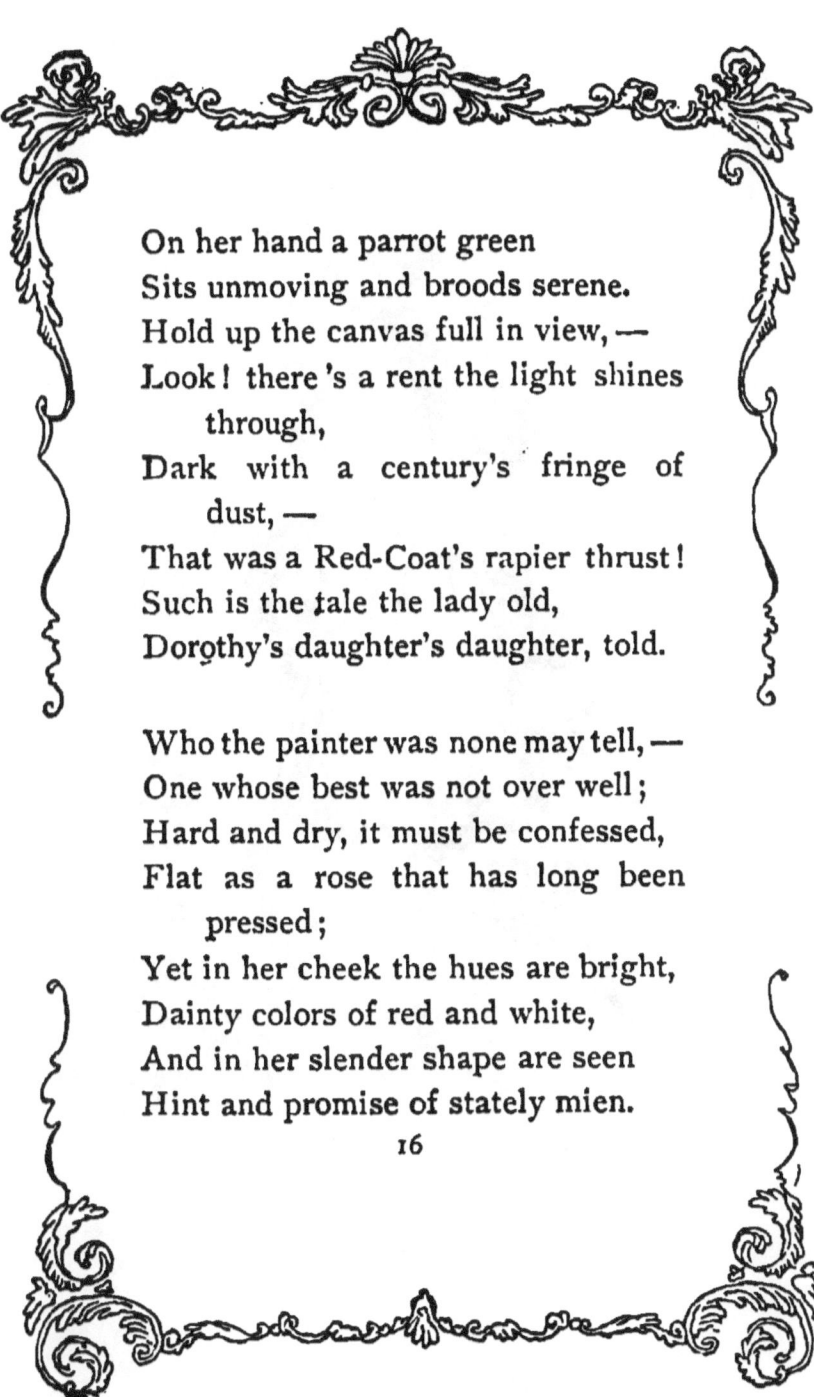

On her hand a parrot green
Sits unmoving and broods serene.
Hold up the canvas full in view, —
Look! there's a rent the light shines
    through,
Dark with a century's fringe of
    dust, —
That was a Red-Coat's rapier thrust!
Such is the tale the lady old,
Dorothy's daughter's daughter, told.

Who the painter was none may tell, —
One whose best was not over well;
Hard and dry, it must be confessed,
Flat as a rose that has long been
    pressed;
Yet in her cheek the hues are bright,
Dainty colors of red and white,
And in her slender shape are seen
Hint and promise of stately mien.

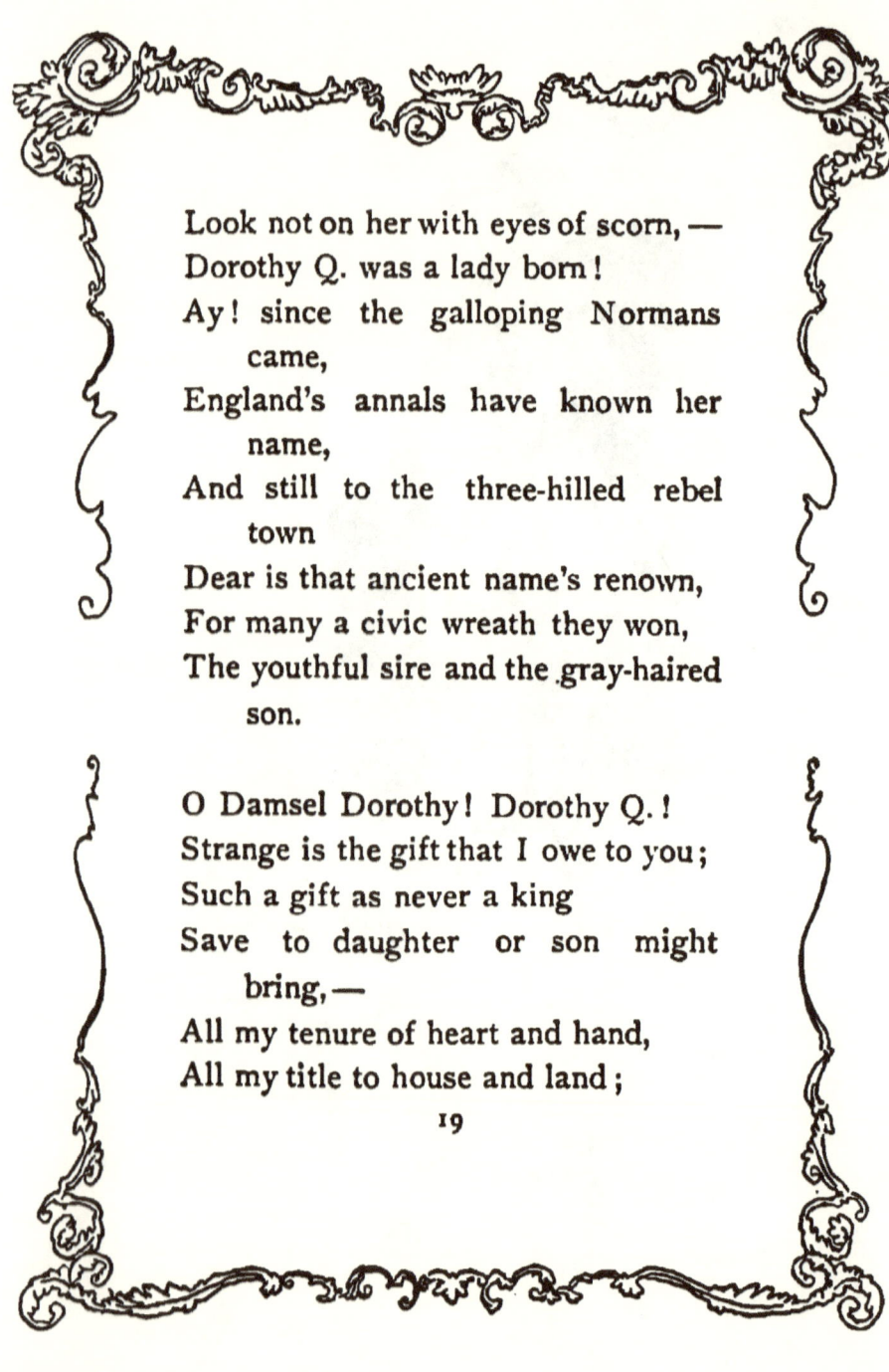

Look not on her with eyes of scorn, —
Dorothy Q. was a lady born!
Ay! since the galloping Normans
    came,
England's annals have known her
    name,
And still to the three-hilled rebel
    town
Dear is that ancient name's renown,
For many a civic wreath they won,
The youthful sire and the gray-haired
    son.

O Damsel Dorothy! Dorothy Q. !
Strange is the gift that I owe to you;
Such a gift as never a king
Save to daughter or son might
    bring, —
All my tenure of heart and hand,
All my title to house and land;

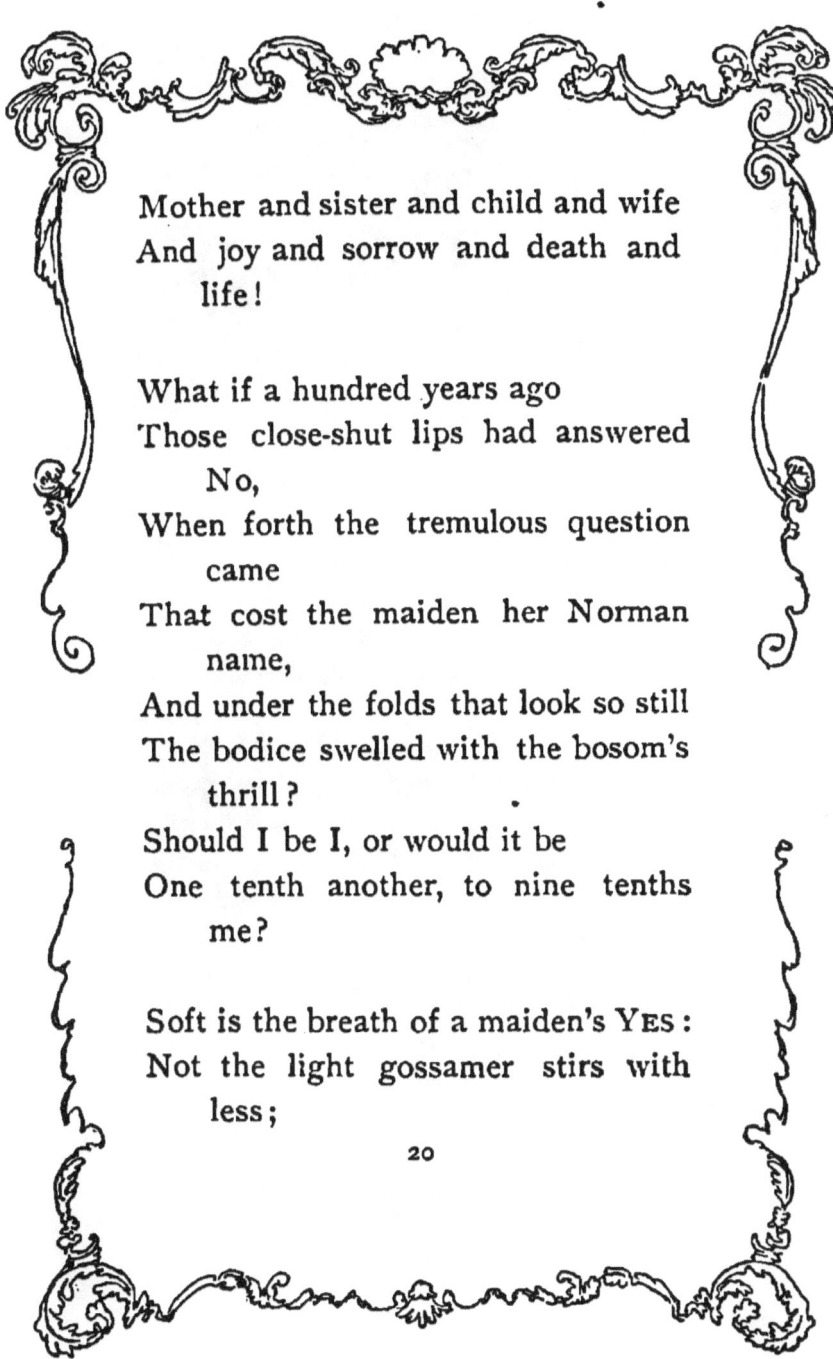

Mother and sister and child and wife
And joy and sorrow and death and
    life!

What if a hundred years ago
Those close-shut lips had answered
    No,
When forth the tremulous question
    came
That cost the maiden her Norman
    name,
And under the folds that look so still
The bodice swelled with the bosom's
    thrill?
Should I be I, or would it be
One tenth another, to nine tenths
    me?

Soft is the breath of a maiden's YES:
Not the light gossamer stirs with
    less;

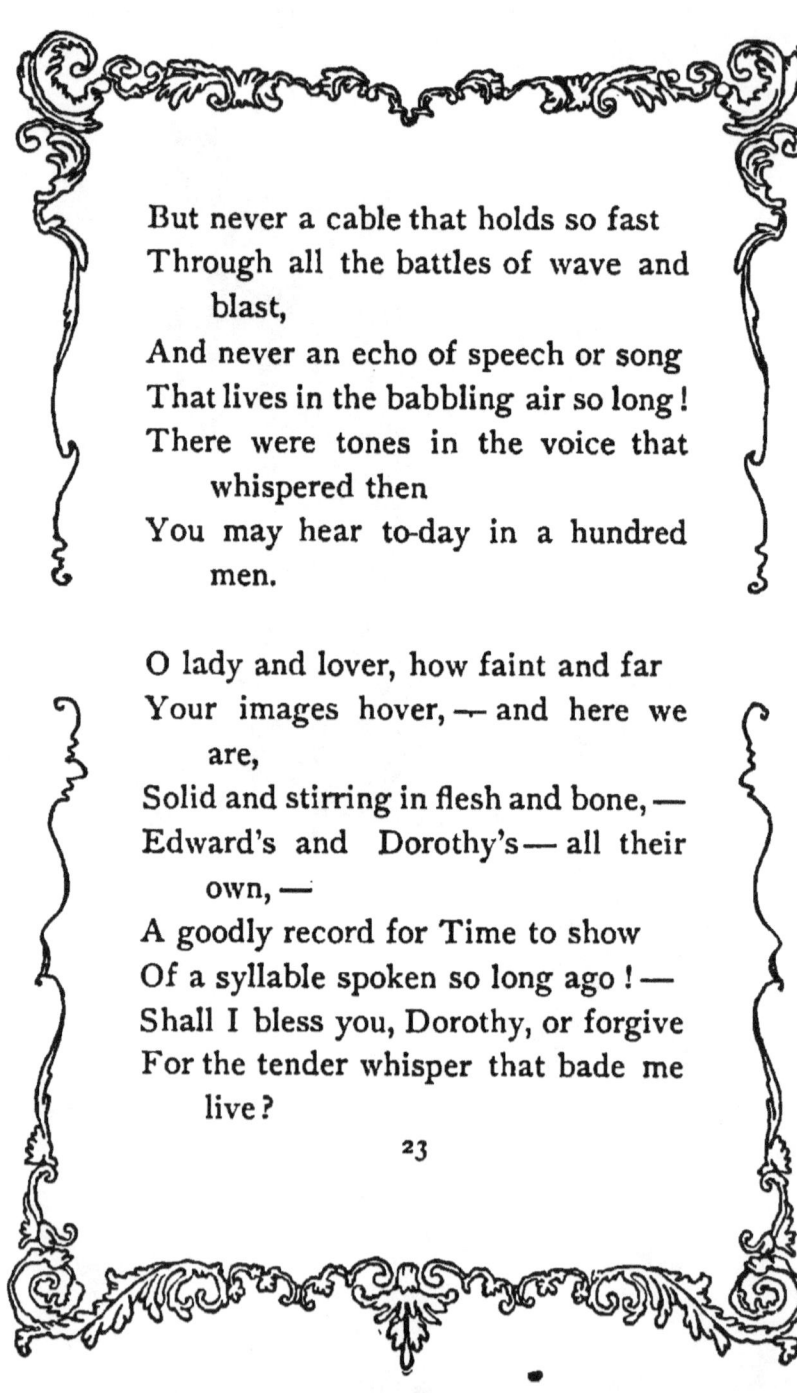

But never a cable that holds so fast
Through all the battles of wave and
blast,
And never an echo of speech or song
That lives in the babbling air so long!
There were tones in the voice that
whispered then
You may hear to-day in a hundred
men.

O lady and lover, how faint and far
Your images hover, — and here we
are,
Solid and stirring in flesh and bone, —
Edward's and Dorothy's — all their
own, —
A goodly record for Time to show
Of a syllable spoken so long ago! —
Shall I bless you, Dorothy, or forgive
For the tender whisper that bade me
live?

23

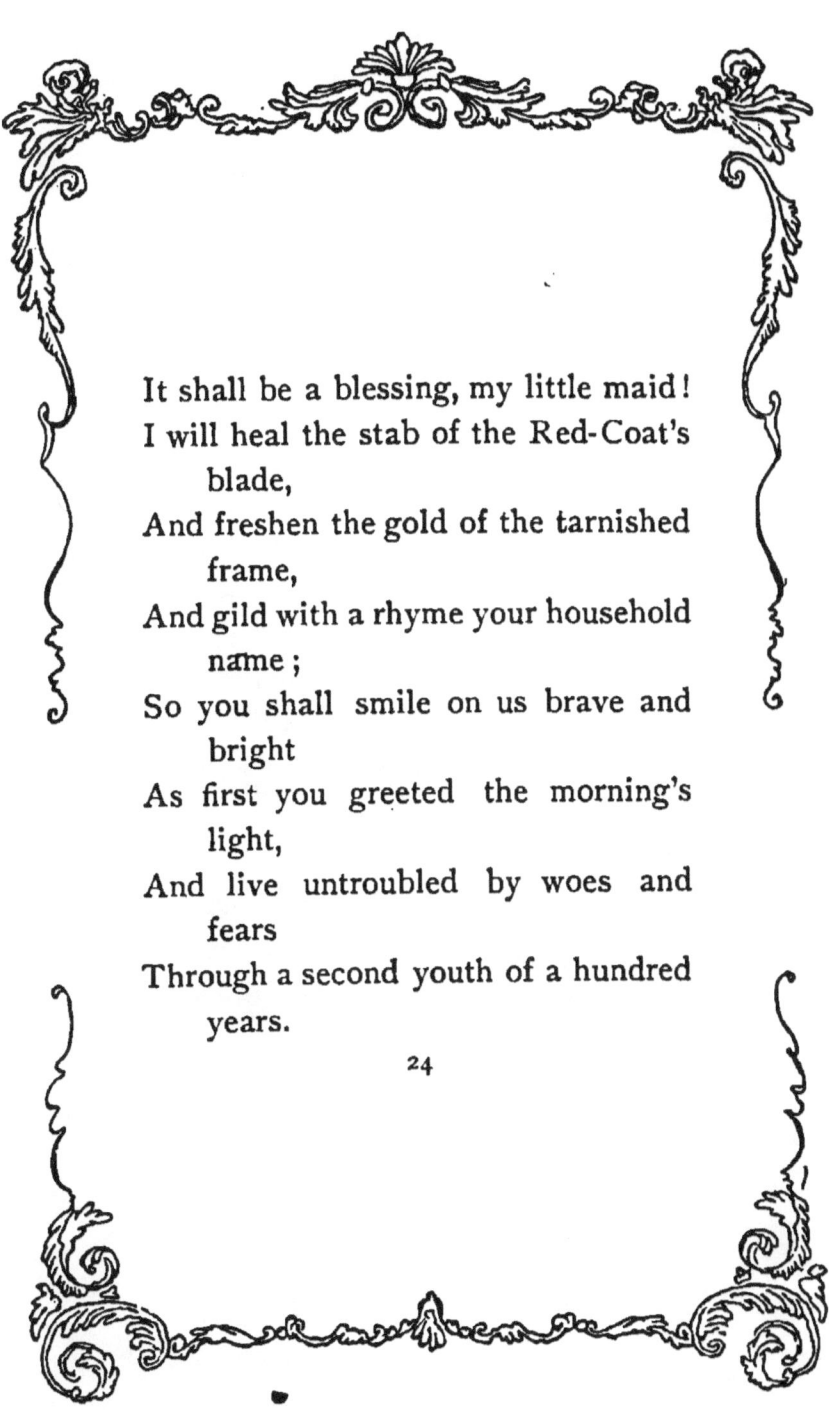

It shall be a blessing, my little maid!
I will heal the stab of the Red-Coat's
blade,
And freshen the gold of the tarnished
frame,
And gild with a rhyme your household
name ;
So you shall smile on us brave and
bright
As first you greeted the morning's
light,
And live untroubled by woes and
fears
Through a second youth of a hundred
years.

24

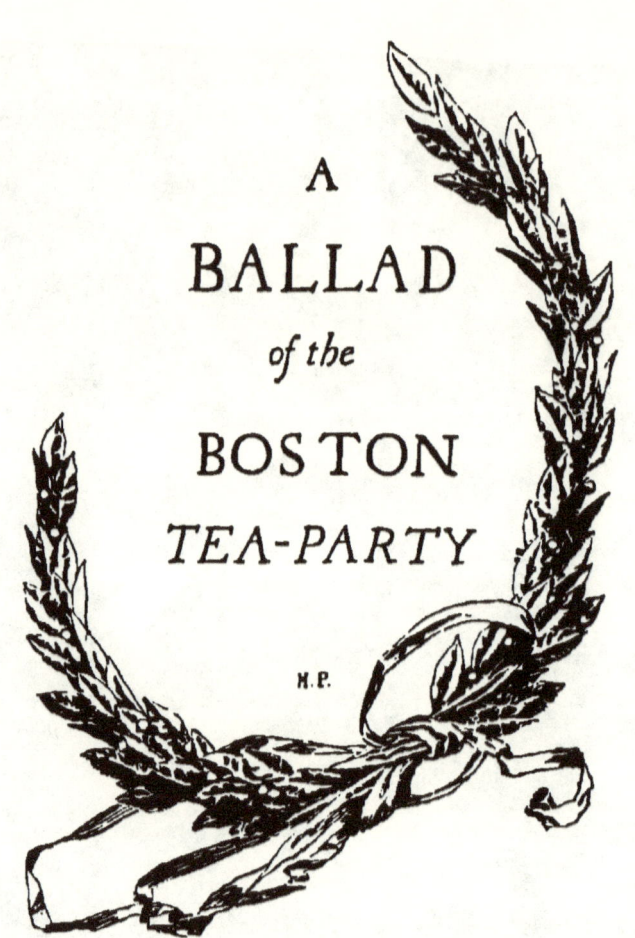

A

BALLAD

of the

BOSTON

TEA-PARTY

H.P.

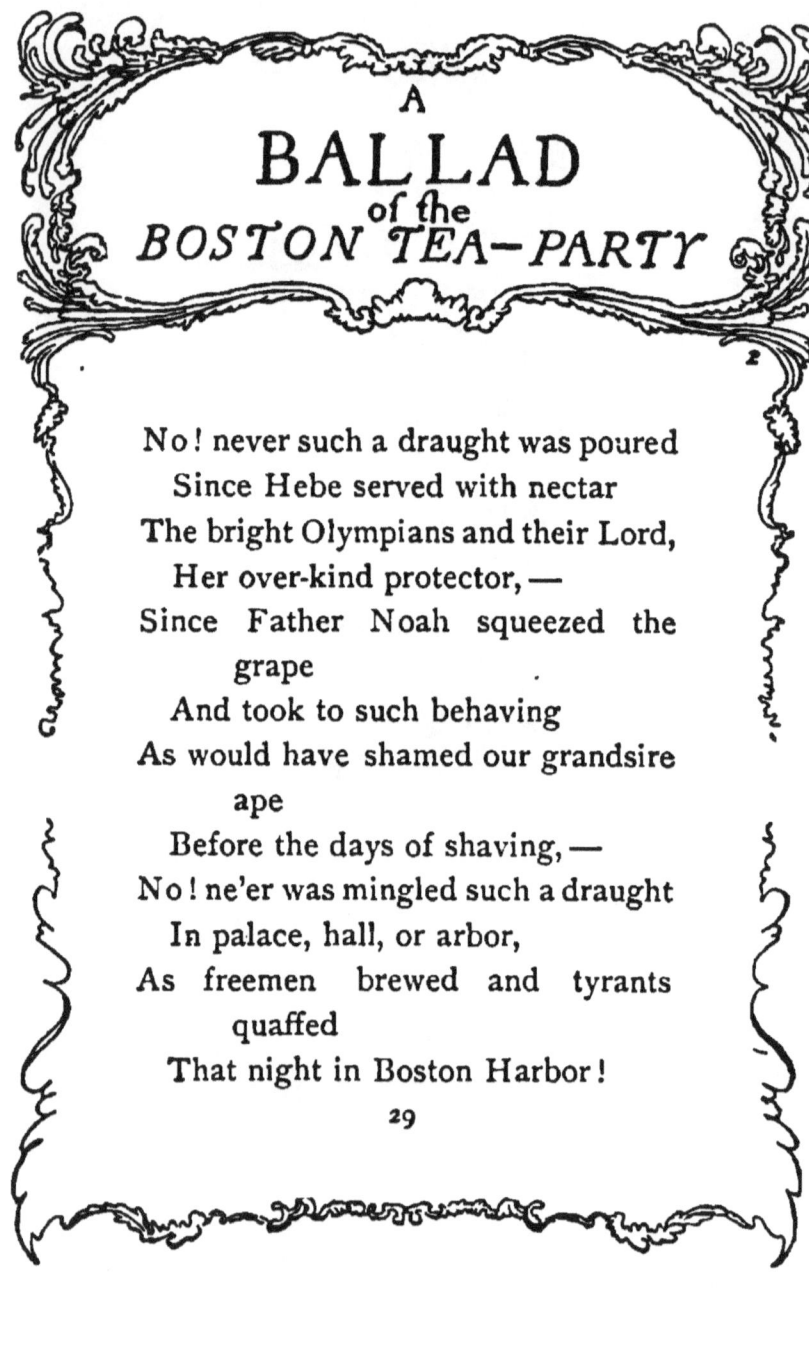

A
BALLAD
of the
BOSTON TEA-PARTY

No! never such a draught was poured
　　Since Hebe served with nectar
The bright Olympians and their Lord,
　　Her over-kind protector, —
Since Father Noah squeezed the
　　grape
　　And took to such behaving
As would have shamed our grandsire
　　ape
　　Before the days of shaving, —
No! ne'er was mingled such a draught
　　In palace, hall, or arbor,
As freemen brewed and tyrants
　　quaffed
　　That night in Boston Harbor!

It kept King George so long awake,
  His brain at last got addled,
It made the nerves of Britain shake,
  With sevenscore millions saddled ;
Before that bitter cup was drained,
  Amid the roar of cannon,
The Western war-cloud's crimson
    stained
  The Thames, the Clyde, the Shan-
    non ;

30

Full many a six-foot grenadier
  The flattened grass had measured,
And many a mother many a year
  Her tearful memories treasured ;
Fast spread the tempest's darkening
     pall,
  The mighty realms were troubled,
The storm broke loose, but first of all
  The Boston teapot bubbled!

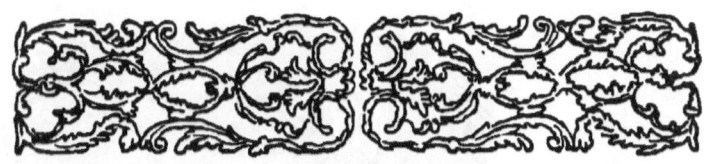

An evening party, — only that,
   No formal invitation,
No gold-laced coat, no stiff cravat,
   No feast in contemplation,
No silk-robed dames, no fiddling band,
   No flowers, no songs, no dancing, —
A tribe of red men, axe in hand, —
   Behold the guests advancing !

34

How fast the stragglers join the
    throng,
From stall and workshop gathered!
The lively barber skips along,
    And leaves a chin half-lathered;

The smith has flung his hammer
  down, —
The horseshoe still is glowing;
The truant tapster at the Crown
Has left a beer-cask flowing;

38

The cooper's boys have dropped the
  adze,
And trot behind their master;
Up run the tarry ship-yard lads, —
The crowd is hurrying faster, —

41

Out from the Millpond's purlieus
    gush
The streams of white-faced millers,
And down their slippery alleys rush
    The lusty young Fort-Hillers;

42

The Fort-Hillers.

The Tories.

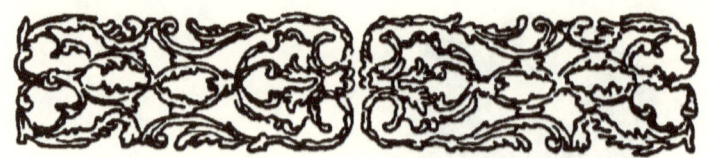

The ropewalk lends its 'prentice
 crew, —
The tories seize the omen :
" Ay, boys, you 'll soon have work to
 do
For England's rebel foemen,
' King Hancock,' Adams, and their
 gang,
That fire the mob with treason, —
When these we shoot and those we
 hang,
The town will come to reason."

45

On — on to where the tea-ships ride!
　And now their ranks are forming, —
A rush, and up the Dartmouth's side
　The Mohawk band is swarming!
See the fierce natives! What a glimpse
　Of paint and fur and feather,
As all at once the full-grown imps
　Light on the deck together!
A scarf the pigtail's secret keeps,
　A blanket hides the breeches, —
And out the cursèd cargo leaps,
　And overboard it pitches!

46

O woman, at the evening board
   So gracious, sweet, and purring,
So happy while the tea is poured,
   So blest while spoons are stirring,
What martyr can compare with thee,
   The mother, wife, or daughter,
That night, instead of best Bohea,
   Condemned to milk and water !

Ah, little dreams the quiet dame
　Who plies with rock and spindle
The patient flax, how great a flame
　Yon little spark shall kindle!
The lurid morning shall reveal
　A fire no king can smother,
Where British flint and Boston steel
　Have flashed against each other!
Old charters shrivel in its track,
　His Worship's bench has crumbled,
It climbs and clasps the union-jack,
　Its blazoned pomp is humbled,
The flags go down on land and sea
　Like corn before the reapers;
So burned the fire that brewed the tea
　That Boston served her keepers!

The waves that wrought a century's
   wreck
   Have rolled o'er whig and tory;
The Mohawks on the Dartmouth's
   deck
   Still live in song and story;
The waters in the rebel bay
   Have kept the tea-leaf savor;
Our old North-Enders in their spray
   Still taste a Hyson flavor;
And Freedom's teacup still o'erflows
   With ever fresh libations,
To cheat of slumber all her foes
   And cheer the wakening nations!

Here endeth

A Ballad

of the

Boston

Tea-Party

H.P.

GRANDMOTHER'S STORY

of

BUNKER HILL BATTLE

•

As she saw it from the

Belfry

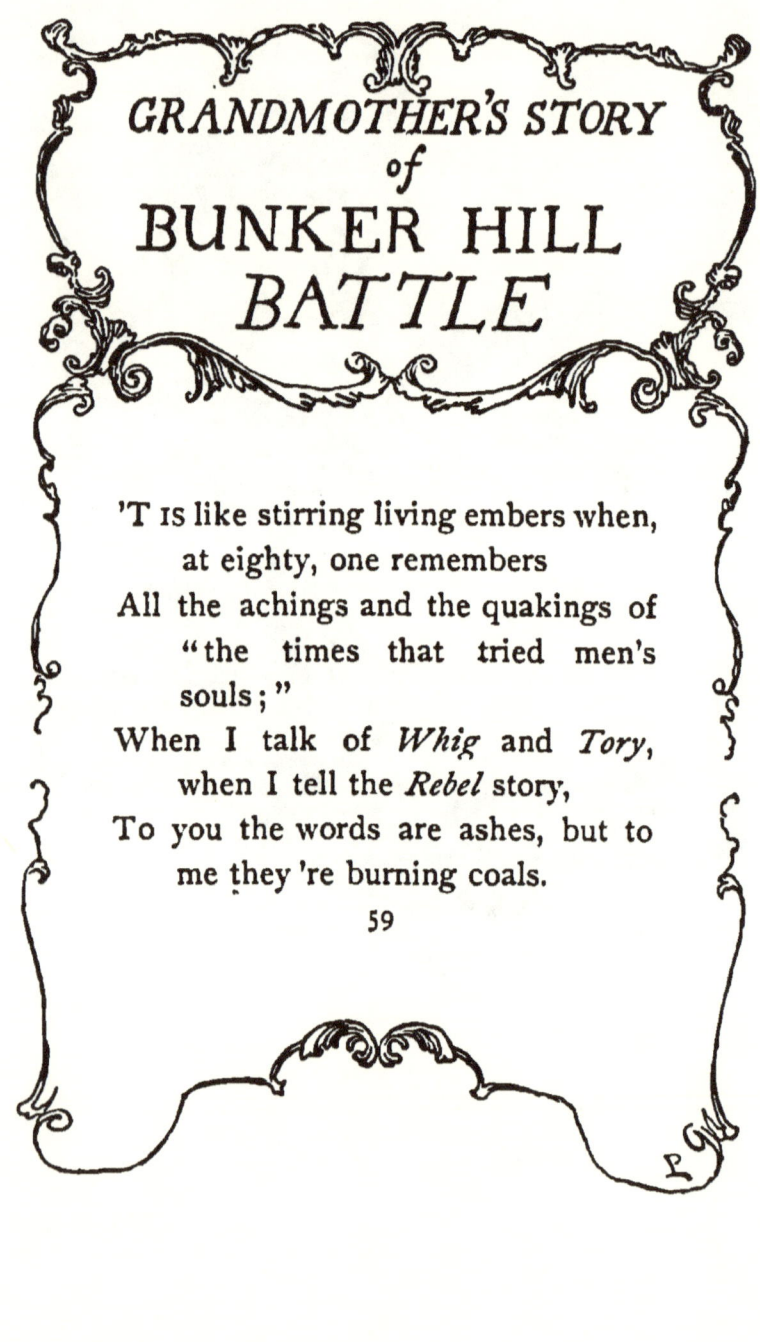

GRANDMOTHER'S STORY
of
BUNKER HILL
BATTLE

'T IS like stirring living embers when,
    at eighty, one remembers
All the achings and the quakings of
    "the times that tried men's
    souls;"
When I talk of *Whig* and *Tory*,
    when I tell the *Rebel* story,
To you the words are ashes, but to
    me they 're burning coals.

I had heard the muskets' rattle of the
    April running battle;
Lord Percy's hunted soldiers, I can
    see their red coats still;
But a deadly chill comes o'er me, as
    the day looms up before me,
When a thousand men lay bleeding
    on the slopes of Bunker's Hill.

60

'T was a peaceful summer's morning,
     when the first thing gave us warn-
     ing
Was the booming of the cannon from
     the river and the shore :
" Child," says grandma, " what 's the
     matter, what is all this noise and
     clatter ?
Have those scalping Indian devils
     come to murder us once more ? "

Poor old soul ! my sides were shaking
    in the midst of all my quaking,
To hear her talk of Indians when the
    guns began to roar :
She had seen the burning village, and
    the slaughter and the pillage,
When the Mohawks killed her father
    with their bullets through his
    door.

64

Then I said, " Now, dear old granny,
  don't you fret and worry any,
For I 'll soon come back and tell you
  whether this is work or play ;
There can't be mischief in it, so I
  won't be gone a minute " —
For a minute then I started. I was
  gone the livelong day.

No time for bodice-lacing or for look-
    ing-glass grimacing;
Down my hair went as I hurried,
    tumbling half-way to my heels;
God forbid your ever knowing, when
    there's blood around her flowing,
How the lonely, helpless daughter of
    a quiet household feels!
68

In the street I heard a thumping; and
I knew it was the stumping
Of the Corporal, our old neighbor, on
that wooden leg he wore,
With a knot of women round him, —
it was lucky I had found him,
So I followed with the others, and the
Corporal marched before.

They were making for the steeple, —
    the old soldier and his people;
The pigeons circled round us as we
    climbed the creaking stair,
Just across the narrow river — oh,
    so close it made me shiver! —
Stood a fortress on the hill-top that
    but yesterday was bare.

Not slow our eyes to find it ; well we
knew who stood behind it,
Though the earthwork hid them from
us, and the stubborn walls were
dumb :
Here were sister, wife, and mother,
looking wild upon each other,
And their lips were white with terror
as they said, THE HOUR HAS
COME !

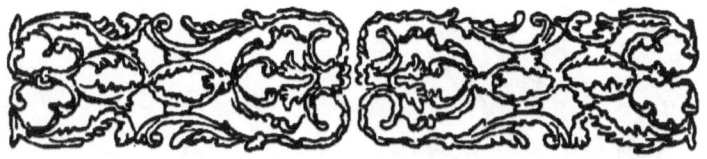

The morning slowly wasted, not a
   morsel had we tasted,
And our heads were almost splitting
   with the cannons' deafening thrill,
When a figure tall and stately round
   the rampart strode sedately;
It was PRESCOTT, one since told me;
   he commanded on the hill.

Every woman's heart grew bigger
    when we saw his manly figure,
With the banyan buckled round it,
    standing up so straight and tall;
Like a gentleman of leisure who is
    strolling out for pleasure,
Through the storm of shells and can-
    non-shot he walked around the
    wall.

79

At eleven the streets were swarming,
    for the red-coats' ranks were
    forming;
At noon in marching order they were
    moving to the piers;
How the bayonets gleamed and glis-
    tened, as we looked far down, and
    listened
To the trampling and the drum-beat
    of the belted grenadiers!

At length the men have started, with
    a cheer (it seemed faint-hearted),
In their scarlet regimentals, with
    their knapsacks on their backs,
And the reddening, rippling water, as
    after a sea-fight's slaughter,
Round the barges gliding onward
    blushed like blood along their
    tracks.

So they crossed to the other border,
    and again they formed in order;
And the boats came back for soldiers,
    came for soldiers, soldiers still:
The time seemed everlasting to us
    women faint and fasting, —
At last they're moving, marching,
    marching proudly up the hill.

84

We can see the bright steel glancing
　　all along the lines advancing —
Now the front rank fires a volley —
　　they have thrown away their shot;
For behind their earthwork lying, all
　　the balls above them flying,
Our people need not hurry; so they
　　wait and answer not.

87

Then the Corporal, our old cripple
    (he would swear sometimes and
     ⁻ tipple), —
He had heard the bullets whistle (in
    the old French war) before, —
Calls out in words of jeering, just as
    if they all were hearing, — ·
And his wooden leg thumps fiercely
    on the dusty belfry floor : —

88

Here lies buried in a
Stone Grave 10 feet deep
Cap DANIEL MALCOM mrch
who departed this Life
october 23d 1769
Aged 44 Years 3
a true son of Liberty
a Friend to the Publick
an Enemy to oppreſsion
and one of the foremoſt
in oppoſing the RevenueActs
on America

"Oh! fire away, ye villains, and earn
    King George's shillin's,
But ye 'll waste a ton of powder afore
    a 'rebel' falls;
You may bang the dirt and welcome,
    they 're as safe as Dan'l Mal-
    colm
Ten foot beneath the gravestone that
    you 've splintered with your
    balls!"

In the hush of expectation, in the
    awe and trepidation
Of the dread approaching moment,
    ˉ we are well-nigh breathless all;
Though the rotten bars are failing on
    the rickety belfry railing,
We are crowding up against them
    like the waves against a wall.

Just a glimpse (the air is clearer),
    they   are   nearer, — nearer, —
    nearer,
When a flash — a curling smoke-
    wreath — then   a   crash — the
    steeple shakes —
The deadly truce is ended; the tem-
    pest's shroud is rended;
Like   a   morning   mist   it   gathered,
    like a thunder-cloud it breaks!

Oh the sight our eyes discover as the
    -blue-black smoke blows over !
The red-coats stretched in windrows
    as a mower rakes his hay;
Here a scarlet heap is lying, there a
    headlong crowd is flying
Like a billow that has broken and is
    shivered into spray.

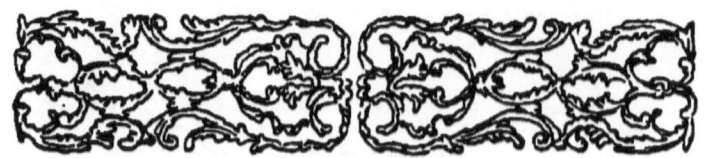

Then we cried, "The troops are
    routed! they are beat — it can't
    be doubted!
God be thanked, the fight is over!"
    — Ah! the grim old soldier's
    smile!
"Tell us, tell us why you look so?"
    (we could hardly speak, we shook
    so), —
"Are they beaten? *Are* they beaten?
    ARE they beaten?" — "Wait a
    while."

Oh the trembling and the terror! for
    too soon we saw our error:
They are baffled, not defeated; we
    have driven them back in vain;
And the columns that were scattered,
    round the colors that were tat-
    tered,
Toward the sullen, silent fortress turn
    their belted breasts again.

All at once, as we are gazing, lo the
    roofs of Charlestown blazing!
They have fired the harmless village;
    in an hour it will be down!
The Lord in heaven confound them,
    rain his fire and brimstone round
    them, —
The robbing, murdering red-coats,
    that would burn a peaceful town!

They are marching, stern and solemn;
   we can see each massive column
As they near the naked earth-mound
   with the slanting walls so steep.
Have our soldiers got faint-hearted,
   and in noiseless haste departed?
Are they panic-struck and helpless?
   Are they palsied or asleep?

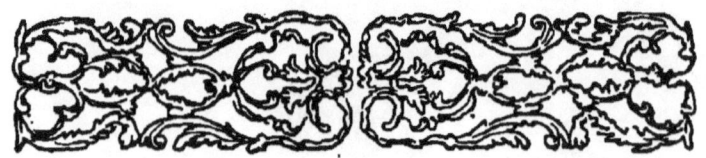

Now! the walls they 're almost under!
scarce a rod the foes asunder!
Not a firelock flashed against them!
up the earthwork they will swarm!
But the words have scarce been spoken, when the ominous calm is
broken,
And a bellowing crash has emptied
all the vengeance of the storm!

So again, with murderous slaughter,
    pelted backwards to the water,
Fly Pigot's running heroes and the
    frightened braves of Howe;
And we shout, " At last they 're done
    for, it 's their barges they have
    run for :
They are beaten, beaten, beaten; and
    the battle 's over now ! "

And we looked, poor timid creatures,
    on the rough old soldier's fea-
    tures,
Our lips afraid to question, but he
    knew what we would ask :
" Not sure," he said ; " keep quiet, —
    once more, I guess, they 'll try
    it —
Here 's damnation to the cut-throats ! "
    — then he handed me his flask,

Saying, " Gal, you 're looking shaky;
    have a drop of old Jamaiky;
I 'm afeard there 'll be more trouble
    afore the job is done; "
So I took one scorching swallow;
    dreadful faint I felt and hollow,
Standing there from early morning
    when the firing was begun.

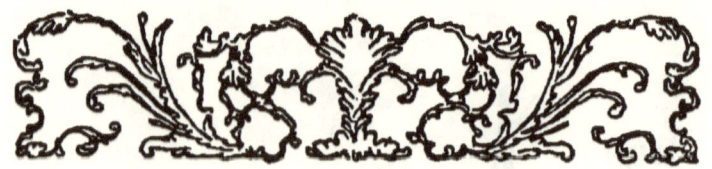

All through those hours of trial I
    had watched a calm clock dial,
As the hands kept creeping, creeping,
    — they were creeping round to
    four,
When the old man said, "They 're
    forming with their bagonets fixed
    for storming :
It 's the death-grip that 's a-coming,
    — they will try the works once
    more."

With brazen trumpets blaring, the
　flames behind them glaring,
The deadly wall before them, in close
　array they come ;
Still onward, upward toiling, like a
　dragon's fold uncoiling, —
Like the rattlesnake's shrill warning
　the reverberating drum !

Over heaps all torn and gory — shall
    I tell the fearful story,
How they surged above the breast-
    work, as a sea breaks over a
    deck;
How, driven, yet scarce defeated, our
    worn-out men retreated,
With their powder-horns all emptied,
    like the swimmers from a wreck?

It has all been told and painted; as
  ⁓for me, they say I fainted,
And the wooden-legged old Corporal
  stumped with me down the stair:
When I woke from dreams affrighted
  the evening lamps were lighted,—
On the floor a youth was lying; his
  bleeding breast was bare.

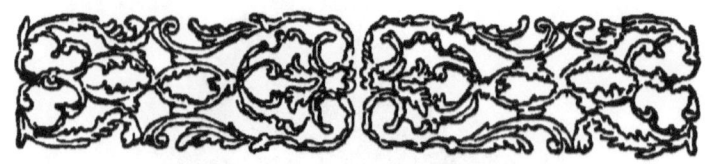

And I heard through all the flurry,
  " Send   for   WARREN ! hurry!
  hurry!
Tell him here's a soldier bleeding,
  and he'll come and dress his
  wound ! "
Ah, we knew not till the morrow told
  its tale of death and sorrow,
How the starlight found him stiffened
  on the dark and bloody ground.

Who the youth was, what his name
　was, where the place from which
　he came was,
Who had brought him from the bat-
　tle, and had left him at our door,
He could not speak to tell us; but
　't was one of our brave fellows,
As the homespun plainly showed us
　which the dying soldier wore.

For they all thought he was dying,
   as they gathered round him cry-
   ing, —
And they said, " Oh, how they 'll miss
   him ! " and " What *will* his
   mother do ? "
Then, his eyelids just unclosing like
   a child's that has been dozing,
He faintly murmured, " Mother ! "
   — and — I saw his eyes were
   blue.

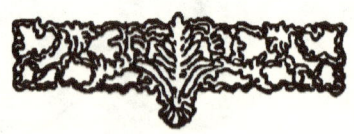

"Why, grandma, how you're wink-
    ing!" Ah, my child, it sets me
    thinking
Of a story not like this one. Well,
    he somehow lived along;
So we came to know each other, and
    I nursed him like a — mother,
Till at last he stood before me, tall,
    and rosy-cheeked, and strong.

And we sometimes walked together
    in the pleasant summer weather,
— " Please to tell us what his name
    was?" Just your own, my little
    dear, —
There's his picture Copley painted:
    we became so well acquainted,
That — in short, that's why I'm
    grandma, and you children all
    are here!"